To Geni
B. A.

To my son, Anton
B. I.

First published 2009 by Walker Books Ltd
87 Vauxhall Walk, London SE11 5HJ

2 4 6 8 10 9 7 5 3 1

Text © 2009 Brian Alderson
Illustrations © 2009 Bagram Ibatoulline

The right of Brian Alderson and Bagram Ibatoulline to be identified as author and illustrator respectively of
this work has been asserted by them in accordance with the Copyright, Designs and Patents Act 1988

This book has been typeset in Centaur.

Printed and bound in China

British Library Cataloguing in Publication Data:
a catalogue record for this book is available from the British Library

ISBN 978-1-4063-2250-7

www.walker.co.uk

HANS CHRISTIAN ANDERSEN

Thumbelina

retold by BRIAN ALDERSON

illustrated by BAGRAM IBATOULLINE

WALKER BOOKS
AND SUBSIDIARIES
LONDON · BOSTON · SYDNEY · AUCKLAND

That's where it all started,
said the swallow.

That's where the woman went off to see
the local witch. She wanted a baby more than
anything and thought the witch could help.
"I don't mind what sort," the woman
said. "I just want a baby."

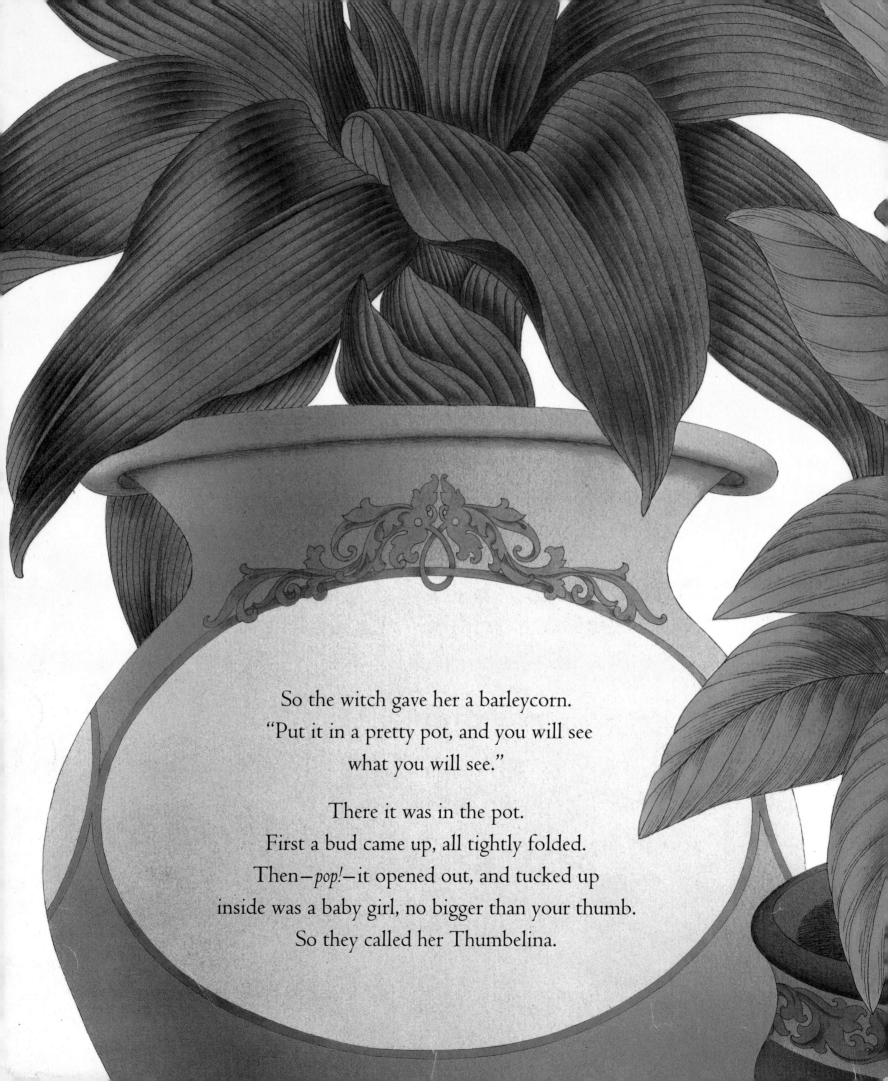

So the witch gave her a barleycorn.
"Put it in a pretty pot, and you will see
what you will see."

There it was in the pot.
First a bud came up, all tightly folded.
Then—*pop!*—it opened out, and tucked up
inside was a baby girl, no bigger than your thumb.
So they called her Thumbelina.

Such a pretty nursery they made for her,
all cosy, there on the windowsill.

Come the spring, and who looks in at the open window
but old Mrs Toad? "*Rek-kek-kek-kek.* What a catchi-
catchi-catch. She shall wed my Toadikins."

She carried Thumbelina out to an eddy in the river
and put her on a lily pad; then she took Thumbelina's
bed down to set up a home with Toadikins in the mud.

Thumbelina wept big tears, but the
river fish heard what was going on, and
they nibbled at the lily pad stalk and...

whisht! away it floated down the river.

My, my, how Thumbelina laughed,
and, when a butterfly joined her on her little boat,
she took off her sash and let the butterfly whiz
her along like a water-skier.

But then—oh, dear—*rrrrrh!* A great big bug came by.
"Here's a pretty thing!" he said, and he carried Thumbelina
off to his tree. (Nobody knows what happened to
the poor butterfly with the sash.)

"Pooh!" said a gaggle of girlie bugs. "Horrid! Look!
Only two legs, no feelers, a skinny little waist! Looks like
a human being." So the bug decided that Thumbelina
wasn't so pretty after all, and he took her down and
dumped her on a daisy.

Bad times then for Thumbelina. She wandered all summer long in the forest, and when autumn came and winter, she could barely keep alive.

But one day there she was at Mrs Fieldmouse's house
begging for a crust of bread. "Oh, you poor, dear thing. Come
in, come in! Why — you can stay here and keep me company.
You can keep the place tidy and do the dishes — and every
day you can tell me a story and I'll teach you to play the flute."

Not long after, Mrs Fieldmouse said she was expecting a visitor: "A well set-up gentleman; he has his own drawing room and a real fur coat. He'll make you a good husband, and, since he can't see to read, you can tell him stories, too."

And there he was at the door: a pompous fellow, winking
and blinking, for he hated the light of day and all the world
that lay above his hole.

He took them along to see his underground mansion.
Halfway there, dead on the floor, was a swallow who hadn't
been able to fly away before the winter came.

The Man in Grey poked his cane through his tunnel roof so that they could see where to tread. "What a rash and heedless fellow that is," he said. "See what happens to you when you go out up there."

Thumbelina was sad about the swallow and secretly brought along a little blanket and some mouse fur to cover the poor thing. But listen! What was that? *Burdum ... burdum ... burdum.* It was a heartbeat, for the swallow wasn't dead but frozen cold.

All winter long she cared for him. She didn't tell Mrs Fieldmouse or the Man in Grey for fear that they would think her foolish, for by this time they had settled on the wedding. The Man in Grey had fallen for Thumbelina's storytelling and her music.

Spring came. The swallow was ready to fly away. "Climb on my back," he said. "Let us both go into the great forest." But Thumbelina wouldn't leave Mrs Fieldmouse and the dishes and the storytelling. "She has been so kind to me," she said. So the swallow flew up alone through the hole in the roof.

But the mouse was not so kind as to forget about the wedding, and all through the summer she made preparations. Thumbelina had to spin the thread for her wedding dress, and four spiders were hired to weave the fabric.

"Now don't be obstropolous," said Mrs Mouse when
Thumbelina moaned about having to live underground.
"Otherwise I shall bite you with my little white teeth. What
a man you've got, with his fur pelisse and all those larders
and drawing rooms!"

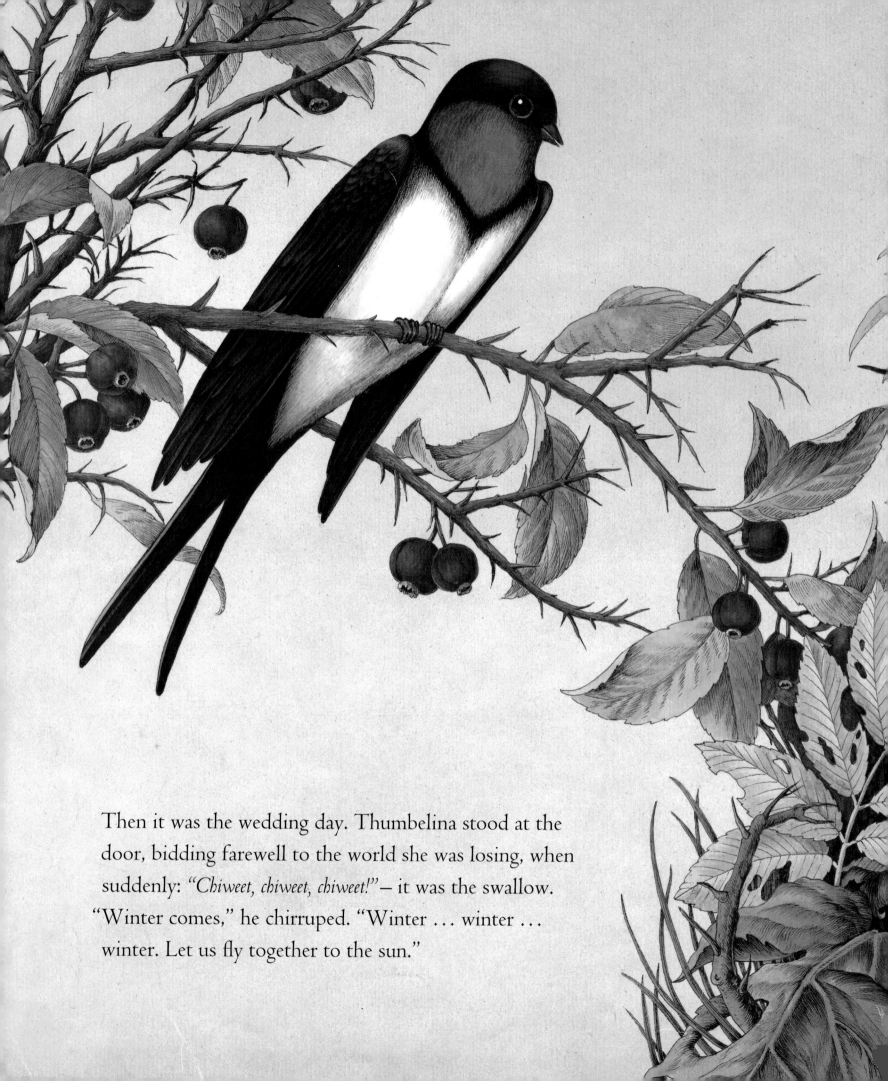

Then it was the wedding day. Thumbelina stood at the
door, bidding farewell to the world she was losing, when
suddenly: *"Chiweet, chiweet, chiweet!"* – it was the swallow.
"Winter comes," he chirruped. "Winter … winter …
winter. Let us fly together to the sun."

That's what they did. Thumbelina climbed onto the
swallow's back, and southwards they flew to the swallow's
summer villa.

No toads or bugs or old grey men there. Only the Crystal
Fairies, dwelling as Thumbelina once had dwelled, in the
buds and blossoms of the flowers.

And there she stayed and married the Crystal King,
while the swallow watched over her and brought her news
every year from the land of her birth. And it is he,
of course, who's been telling you this story.